JUMP!

Scott M. Fischer

SIMON & SCHUSTER BOOKS FOR YOUNG READERS
New York   London   Toronto   Sydney

Well,
I'm a **bug**.
I'm a **bug**.

I'm a snug little **bug**,
and I'm sleeping on a **jug**.

Until I see a **frog,**   and I . . .

JUMP!

Until I see a **cat**,

and I . . .

Well, I'm a **cat**.
I'm a **cat**.

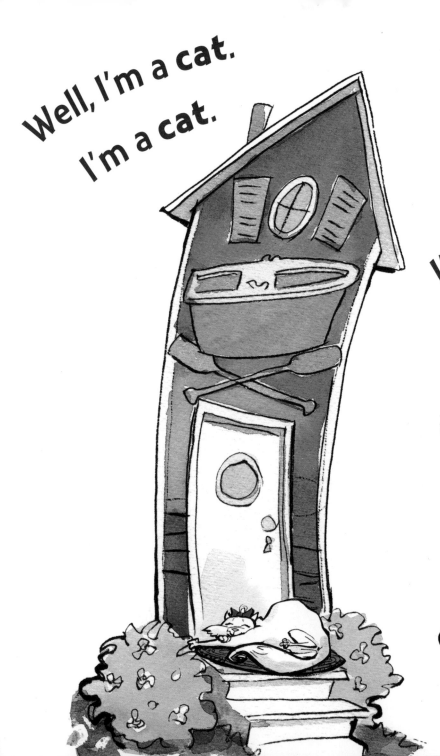

I'm a fat little **cat**,
and I'm sleeping on a **mat**.

Until I see a **hound,**

and I . . .

Until I see a **croc**, and I . . .

Well, I'm a **croc**.
I'm a **croc**.

I'm a croc on a **dock**,
and I'm sleeping like a **rock**.

Until I see a **shark**, and I . . .

Well, I'm a shark.
I'm a shark.
My teeth spark in the dark.
I don't sleep 'cause I'm a shark.

But when I see a
whale,
I . . .

Well, I'm a whale.
I'm a whale.

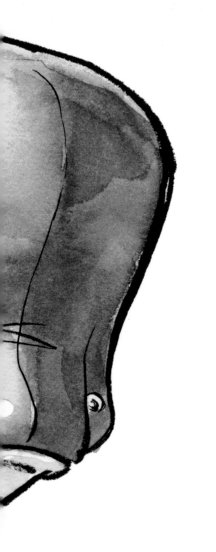

I'm a whale setting sail,
and it's time to end this tale!

Dedicated to little Sarah, the original Jumpinator!

ACKNOWLEDGMENTS

To Teresa, Ang, Kev, Eddie, and Laurent, who have jumped to the moon and back for me many times.

To Mom and Dad, for encouraging me to jump as high as I could.

To Dotty and the Renaissance School, for all jumping like popcorn!

And thanks to my fellow rocker Rick, who said, "That song should be a book!"

Want to hear the song that started it all? Go to fischart.com/KidsMusic.html and put your JUMPING shoes on!

SIMON & SCHUSTER BOOKS FOR YOUNG READERS
An imprint of Simon & Schuster Children's Publishing Division ▪ 1230 Avenue of the Americas, New York, New York 10020
Copyright © 2010 by Scott M. Fischer ▪ All rights reserved, including the right of reproduction in whole or in part in any form.
SIMON & SCHUSTER BOOKS FOR YOUNG READERS is a trademark of Simon & Schuster, Inc.
For information about special discounts for bulk purchases, please contact Simon & Schuster Special Sales at 1-866-506-1949 or business@simonandschuster.com.
The Simon & Schuster Speakers Bureau can bring authors to your live event.
For more information or to book an event, contact the Simon & Schuster Speakers Bureau at 1-866-248-3049 or visit our website at www.simonspeakers.com.

Book design by Laurent Linn
The text for this book is set in Montara Gothic. ▪ The illustrations for this book are rendered in watercolor.
Manufactured in China
2 4 6 8 10 9 7 5 3 1

MAR 2 6 2010

Library of Congress Cataloging-in-Publication Data
Fischer, Scott M.
Jump! / Scott Fischer.—1st ed.
p. cm.
Summary: From bugs and frogs to alligators and whales, frightened animals always move out of the way of a larger opponent.
ISBN: 978-1-4169-7884-8
[1. Stories in rhyme. 2. Animals—Fiction. 3. Fear—Fiction.] I. Title.
PZ8.3.F6286Ju 2010   [E]—dc22   2008025861

first edition